Max and Zoe

at the Doctor's

by Shelley Swanson Sateren
illustrated by Mary Sullivan

raintree
a Capstone company — publishers for children

Raintree is an imprint of Capstone Global Library Limited, a
company incorporated in England and Wales having its registered
office at 264 Banbury Road, Oxford, OX2 7DY – Registered
company number: 6695582

www.raintree.co.uk
myorders@raintree.co.uk

Designed by Emily Harris
Production by Katy LaVigne
Originated by Capstone Global Library Ltd
Printed and bound in India

ISBN 978 1 4747 9063 5 (hardback)
ISBN 978 1 4747 9069 7 (paperback)

British Library Cataloguing in Publication Data
A full catalogue record for this book is available from
the British Library.

Contents

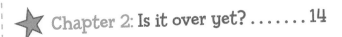
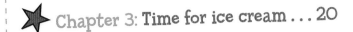

Chapter 1
Now that hurts!

Max and Zoe were at the park.

"We need to practise our gymnastics," said Max.

"I know," said Zoe. "We've got our lesson tomorrow."

Zoe did a cartwheel and a headstand.

Max did a round-off. He landed by doing the splits.

"Wow!" said Zoe. "Did that hurt?"

"Not at all," Max said. "You try."

Zoe did a round-off. She landed by doing the splits too.

"We should start a club, Zoe," said Max. "Our club could be called The Banana Splits!"

"Cool!" said Zoe.

Max and Zoe did splits after splits.

"Wow!" said a boy. "Does
that hurt?"

"Not at all," Max said.

"Max and Zoe!" called
Mum. "Time to go."

"Hooray!" Max
yelled. "Time for ice
cream!"

Max was so excited! He jumped up on the wall. He did a cartwheel, right on top! Suddenly, Max's hand slid off the wall.

He fell towards the grass.

His leg hit a sharp rock.

"Ouch!" yelled Max.

"Oh no!" said Zoe.

"You've cut your leg."

"Now that hurts," said

Max.

"That's a bad cut," said

Mum. "You need to see a

doctor. Ice cream will have

to wait."

"Will Max need stitches?"

Zoe asked.

"I don't know," said Mum.

"I had stitches on my chin once," said Zoe. "The doctor sewed the cut together."

Max had seen Zoe's grandma sewing. The needle was sharp.

"I don't want stitches!" Max said.

Chapter 2
Is it over yet?

At the clinic, Max sat on a table. Mum held his hand.

"You need stitches," said the doctor. He cleaned around the cut. "I'll give you an injection. Then you won't feel the pain."

The injection was over quickly. The doctor washed the cut with water. He wiped out the dirt.

That part didn't hurt. But would the stitches?

The doctor put some
thread into a needle.

"Oh no," said Max.

"Don't look," said Zoe.

"Watch me!"

Zoe did the splits. Max
watched.

"Wow!" said a nurse.

"When will it be over?"

asked Max.

"Soon," said the doctor.

Zoe did a headstand. Max watched.

"Is it over yet?" he asked.

"Almost," said the doctor.

Zoe's legs stayed up and up and up!

"That's your longest headstand ever!" said Max.

"All done," said the doctor. "Seven stitches."

"It's done!" Max said.

"Good!" Zoe's legs dropped at last.

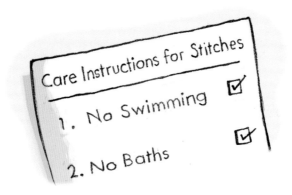

"Your stitches will come out in one week," said the nurse. "Until then, keep your leg dry. No swimming."

"Oh," Max said with a frown.

"And no baths," the nurse said.

"Great!" Max said with a smile. "Now it's time for ice cream!"

At the ice cream shop,

Max was tired but hungry.

Max said to the lady,

"I've had seven stitches!"

"Wow!" said the lady.

"That calls for a special

treat."

Max pointed to a sign.

"That's what I want."

"Me too!" said Zoe.

"Banana splits!" they yelled together.

"You split your chin open," said Max. "I split my leg. We really are The Banana Splits!"

"A perfect ending to a crazy day," Zoe said.

About the author

Shelley Swanson Sateren is the award-winning author of many children's books. She has worked as a children's book editor and in a children's bookshop. Today, as well as writing, Shelley works with primary-school-aged children in various settings. She lives in Minnesota, USA, with her husband and two sons.

About the illustrator

Mary Sullivan has been drawing and writing all her life, which has mostly been spent in Texas, USA. She earned a BFA from the University of Texas in Studio Art.

Glossary

cartwheel a sideways flip with arms and legs held straight out

headstand holding yourself upright on your head with the help of your hands

injection medicine given through a needle into the skin

round-off an act similar to a cartwheel that ends with both legs finishing together at the same time

splits to slide to the floor with your legs spread in opposite directions

stitches a way to close up a wound

Discussion questions

1. Would you like to do gymnastics? Why or why not?

2. Why is it important to go to the doctor if you are hurt?

3. Zoe helps distract Max while he's at the doctor. If you had to go to the doctor, who would you want to go with you? Why?

Hi MAX!

Writing Prompts

1. Max and Zoe name their club The Banana Splits. Make up your own club and make a poster for it. Make sure you include your club's name and its purpose.

2. It's important to stay safe when you are playing. Make a list of three playground rules.

3. Zoe is a good friend to Max. Write a few sentences about one of your good friends.

Make your own banana split

What you need:

- butter knife
- chopping board
- spoon
- ice cream scoop
- long bowl or a deep, oval dish
- 1 scoop each of vanilla, chocolate and strawberry ice cream
- one banana
- sprinkles
- chocolate sauce
- strawberry ice cream topping
- or fresh strawberries
- crushed nuts
- whipped cream
- 3 cherries

What you do:

1. Put one scoop of each flavour ice cream in a row in the bowl or dish.

2. Peel the banana. With adult help, slice the banana in half the long way.

3. Press the "split" banana halves onto each side of the ice cream row.

4. Top the vanilla ice cream with the sprinkles.

5. Top the chocolate ice cream with the chocolate sauce.

6. Top the strawberry ice cream with strawberry sauce or fresh strawberries.

7. Cover all of the scoops of ice cream with crushed nuts.

8. Top each scoop with some whipped cream.

9. Put a cherry on top of each scoop.

Now enjoy your tasty treat!

The fun doesn't stop here!

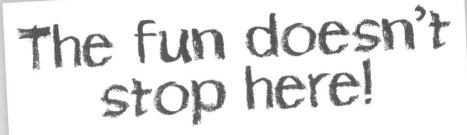

We have lots more Max and Zoe adventures for you to enjoy!

Discover more books and favourite characters at
www.raintree.co.uk